CW01668516

DAVID

KEYS TO DIVINE HEALTH

KEYS TO DIVINE HEALTH

ISBN 978-978-2480-28-6

Reprinted Reprinted 1993, 1994, 1995, 1998, 2001, 2004, 2007, 2008, 2009, 2010, 2016, 2017, 2022
Re-edited: 2023

Published in Nigeria by

DOMINION PUBLISHING HOUSE

For further information or permission, address:

Km 10, Idiroko Road, Canaanland, Ota, Nigeria.

Tel: +234 816 406 0777, +234 909 151 4022

Or visit our website: www.dphprints.com

Connect with David O. Oyedepo

David Oyedepo Ministries International *@davidoyedepomin*

@davidoyedepomin *faithtabernacle.org.ng*

Connect with Living Faith Church via

Living Faith Church Worldwide

faithtabernacle.org.ng

All Scripture quotations are from the King James Version of the Bible, except otherwise stated.

Contents

Introduction

The Word of God stands steadfast forever. It does not and cannot change. It is the eternal Word. God and His Word are one. You cannot separate Him from His Word. He is as eternal as His Word. Whatsoever will change God's Word must change God Himself and God cannot change. He said,

I am the LORD, I change not...

Malachi 3:6

As you go through this book, determine to get the best out of it. You may be used to some of the facts expressed here, but they are God's divine provisions revealed in His Word to you, to change your situations.

The Lord Jesus Christ came into the world, primarily, to make life much more fulfilling and exciting for us. Everything He went through and accomplished was for us collectively. It was for us He came. He came to set us free from all forms of problems — sin, sickness, disease, poverty, and all evils of this present world.

> ***Grace be to you and peace from God the Father, and from our Lord Jesus Christ,***
>
> ***Who gave himself for our sins, that he might deliver us from this present evil world, according to the will of God and our Father:***
>
> *Galatians 1:3-4*

This is a brief summary of the ministry of Jesus, while He was here on earth. He came to give us abundant life, and all things that make for life and godliness.

Nobody really wants to be sick. There is an innate desire and deep hunger to be in health, and I believe this is your own true situation. You really want to be healthy! That is exactly what this book is all about. It will show you the way to living healthy and abiding in divine health.

Before you go on, make this confession in

faith. Remember Jesus said, you can have what you say (Mark 11:23).

'Heavenly Father, in the name of Jesus, I open my heart today to receive Your Word. I know your Word has the power to transform. So, as I read this book, my life is transformed from glory to glory. Sicknesses and diseases shall begin to flee from me. From now, I will live like Jesus—free from all oppression, enjoying every part of my body, in Jesus name! Amen.

1

Jesus, Our Pattern

The first thing I want you to consider seriously is the life of the Lord Jesus Christ. This is necessary so we can have a solid foundation.

The Bible tells us in many ways that Jesus is our example. He is the author and finisher of our faith. He is the final pattern in all matters that relate to believers. He is the 'Pattern Son'.

> ***Looking unto Jesus the author and finisher of our faith...***
>
> *Hebrews 12:2*

God's ultimate goal is to bring us to the full stature of Christ in every aspect of life (Ephesians 4:13).

Taking a careful look and diligent study of the gospels of Matthew, Mark, Luke and

John, it is expressly clear that the Lord Jesus Christ did not fall sick at any time. He was constantly sound, strong, hale and hearty. His health did not deteriorate for a second. He was a divine symbol of God's will in healthy living on earth.

Hebrews 12:2 tells us that Jesus Christ is our target of faith. He is our target in all matters, including health. He is our pattern in God's health programme.

This explains why we do not argue or contest perfection. If Jesus knew no sin while in the body on earth, and He is our pattern of faith, there is no point arguing against it. If we do not contest sinless perfection, there is no justification for any argument against a sickness-free body.

In God's scheme of things, we are not expected to accommodate any form of sickness in our bodies. The point is that, Jesus is our perfect example. He is our target of faith. We are permitted, based on our redemptive rights to claim by faith any benefit we can see in the life of Christ. We can get it. It is God's provision for us.

It is pathetic to note that despite God's revelation to man on the subject of health, many of His precious people are still under the yoke of sicknesses and diseases. Many even seem to believe it is God's will for them to be sick, while some take solace in medical science. Such is the deceit of the devil.

God has made a sickness-free provision for all His people and He wants us to know that and walk in it.

A lot of people, instead of staying healthy are constantly expecting 'their sickness' so that they can run to the pastor or an anointed man of God to receive their healing. They are still babes! They cannot stand on the sickness-free covenant with God and stay healthy. You do not need to continue looking for healing anywhere; you have to go beyond that.

Jesus, in conversing with the woman of Canaan, made a statement of fact concerning healing and health. She wanted Jesus to heal her daughter, who was vexed with an evil spirit. But Jesus said to her, *...It is not meet to* *take the children's bread, and to cast it to dogs* (Matthew 15:26).

He said healing is children's bread! Note that the Word says, 'children's bread', not 'son's bread'. Sons (grown-ups in the faith), do not need healing. They have gone beyond that, they are in health, and they know their right to health; but children still need healing,

> ***Now I say, That the heir, as long as he is a child, differeth nothing from a servant, though he be lord of all;***
>
> ***Even so we, when we were children, were in bondage under the elements of the world:***
>
> ***But when the fulness of the time was come, God sent forth his Son, made of a woman, made under the law,***
>
> ***To redeem them that were under the law, that we might receive the adoption of sons.***
>
> *Galatians 4:1, 3-5*

If unbelievers get sick and get healed their own way and as a believer, you too get sick and get healed your own way; then, the Word says you are not different from a servant. This implies that if you will take your proper place as a son, God will also take His place as a Father, and when sonship consciousness gets into you, sickness is forgotten.

The sonship stage is when we have outgrown childhood or infancy. We are no longer babes in Christ. At this stage of growth, we are fully enlightened and consciously aware of our rights and privileges. At sonship, you stop seeing things as being at God's disposal. You now know that whatever you get or do not get is your own decision. You now know what God must do and why He must do it; you are no longer a child but a son.

The heart of the matter is the fact that God has no plans for you to be sick, just as He had no plans for Jesus to be sick. In God's plan, you and Jesus are not different. He is the pattern Son. He is the firstborn (Colossians 1:15,18) and we are His brethren. God sees us as such. In fact, the Lord Jesus Himself indicated this. He was so plain about it. He said,

Verily, verily, I say unto you, He that

> ***believeth on me, the works that I do shall he do also; and greater works than these shall he do; because I go unto my Father.***
>
> *John 14:12*

You have everything that Jesus had when He was in the body. There is no secret about it, you are complete in Him. So, it is your own responsibility to make them real in your life. It is absolutely possible to live without sicknesses and diseases. That is divine health.

Jesus lived in it and we can do the same too. By the time you get into this, you will no longer be talking about healing; you will be talking health. The devil will respect you fully and will be full of fear, because you know your right to health.

I read the story of a woman who got hold of the Word on divine health at the age of 35. Her life was literally transformed; she lived a life free from the least headache and went to be with the Lord at 94.

She knew she did not need to be sick. In fact, she still washed her plates in her kitchen on the day she died. She was very healthy. She was no nuisance to those living with and around her. She was as strong as she had always been.

There are many people today, who are merely 60 years old, and are already giving their people serious concern. Their systems have degenerated and they are as good as dead. But divine health guarantees strength, even at old age.

In the days of the apostles, sickness among believers was not common. It was not normal for a believer to be sick. There was no precedent for it. There is no account about the apostles that indicates that any of them was sick at any time. They were constantly in health.

Even Thomas who seemed to be lacking in faith walked in sound health all the time! Judas, as long as he walked with Jesus was also sound in health. Jesus did not only walk in health; He made His environment healthy. His presence was enough to sanctify His disciples from sickness!

This explains why James had to write

asking, 'Is there any sick among you?' It was not common to be sick then. Sickness is not part of the body of Christ. Sound health is for the body of Christ, while sickness is one of the elements of the body of satan—the kingdom of darkness. So, James asked, 'Is it likely that there is any sick there?'

The Church is superior to sickness. It is not for us. This is why it was easy for Paul to identify the reason some Christians in the Corinthian Church were sickly and weak. He knew it was not normal, not conventional. It was as a result of something. Paul said the reason was that they took the blood and body of the Lord unworthily, not discerning the body.

> ***For he that eateth and drinketh unworthily, eateth and drinketh damnation to himself, not discerning the Lord's body.***
>
> ***FOR THIS CAUSE many are weak and sickly among you, and many sleep.***
>
> *1 Corinthians 11:29-30 (Emphasis Mine)*

Paul states here that the reason God's

people were weak and sickly was because of Holy Communion taken unworthily. But the situation today is not so. People are sick because of their ignorance of God's provision for their health.

From James' statement, it is conclusive that health is of great importance to God. It is clear that He would overlook sin to heal a believer, and forgive him in the process.

> ***Is any sick among you? let him call for the elders of the church; and let them pray over him...***
>
> ***And the prayer of faith shall save the sick, and the Lord shall raise him up; and if he have committed sins, they shall be forgiven him.***
>
> *James 5:14-15*

God seems to be saying, 'I hate to see My people sick. Even if they have sinned, I will forgive them'.

This may sound like God is slack about sin, but He is not! He is expressing the strong emphasis He has placed on our health, and He will do anything to make sure our health is guaranteed. He wants and intends for His family to be a symbol of divine health.

He is saying, 'Do not nurse, accommodate or entertain that sickness in your body. As small as it may be, call on the elders. Let them pray for you that you may be restored to health. Even if there is any obstacle, sin or whatever, I will take care of it. Just let him be healed'.

2

Our Rights To Health

Our God-given, purchased and guaranteed rights to health is expressly stated in His Word. He openly declared His plan for our being in health so clearly, that it is easily understandable.

God entered into a covenant relationship with His people under the Old Testament. One of such covenants is the covenant of good health.

> ***And ye shall serve the LORD your God, and he shall bless thy bread, and thy water; and I will take sickness away from the midst of thee.***
>
> *Exodus 23:25*

As long as we are in God's service, sickness, disease, affliction and any such evil shall not and cannot have dominion over us.

Note that He said, *I will take sickness away from the midst of thee.* God will take it away from you. If sickness is taken away, all you have left is health! That is divine health.

There are many things involved in that passage of scripture. It is a four-term contract.

You shall serve the Lord your God:

He shall bless your bread;

He shall bless your water;

And He shall take sickness away from the midst of thee.

Everyone involved in God's service is entitled to divine health. Are you in His service? Sickness has been removed from you. In God's mind, you are in health. The term of the contract is service to God. If that is carried out, God has taken care of His own side of it. If you are faithful, God is ever faithful.

... but a faithful ambassador is health.

Proverbs 13:17

A faithful servant of God is healthy. That means he is an embodiment of health. We are all ambassadors of Christ (2 Corinthians 5:20); therefore, health is ours by right. It is not a special favour from God. It is not for a selected few. It is for you by right—on covenant basis.

God has a duty to make us healthy and stay so. He has made everything available to guarantee our health. However, it is our responsibility to walk into it and enjoy it.

The fulfilment of this covenant of health was clearly manifested in the lives of the people of Israel, the Church in the wilderness (Acts 7:38). They moved with God and served Him. As long as they obeyed God and were in His service, He upheld the covenant of health He had earlier made with them.

> ***He brought them forth also with silver and gold: and there was not one feeble (weak, sick) person among their tribes.***
>
> *Psalm 105:37 (Paraphrased)*

The Psalmist is talking about the Church in the wilderness. He is giving an account of how God brought them out with strength and throughout their 40 years journey, there was no sick person among their tribes. Sickness had no entrance into their midst.

Note that this was for the Church in the wilderness, under the ministration of death, with the old covenant. If the ministration of death could be that glorious, such that there was no feeble person among all their tribes, how much more shall the ministration of life excel in glory.

The figurative Church had no sickness. The real body —the Church of the Lord Jesus Christ should not have any such thing! The Bible says that Jesus Christ was the Rock that followed them in the wilderness. He was with them as a Rock, He is now with us as the Living Saviour. The risen and glorified Christ is with the New Testament Church. He is exalted and set on the right hand of Majesty on high. God's divine purpose for the Church is to stay in divine health.

In the beginning, we are told that God created man and everything that was necessary, and He saw that it was very good. But do you ever notice that God did not provide a means for healing?

He created His man, put him in charge of everything He had made, and provided no means of getting healed. The reason was that when God created His man, He made him in His own very image, immune to any form of sickness. In fact, man had no sickness or disease-consciousness. So, that man (Adam) did not need healing.

God did not provide for healing because they (Adam and Eve) were not made to be sick. He knew they needed food, so He provided everything for food; none of those things were made for drugs. Their creation was made drug-free.

The Entrance of Sickness

There are three areas through which sickness entered into the world. The first is sin. There was no sickness in the world until Adam sinned. Before this time, Adam was in a state of perfect and absolute health; he did not know sickness. He was always strong, hale and hearty. There was no symptom of headache or fever.

It was when he sinned that sickness came in. An unregenerate man is not entitled to divine health. The Bible says that man has sinned and come short of the glory of God (Romans 3:23). Man cannot enjoy divine health except the sin problem is dealt with. There is no way a man that is sin-ridden can enjoy divine health. He has to first submit himself to Jesus Christ, then he will have access to God's provision of divine health.

There was no sickness before sin, and if sickness must leave, sin, the root cause must go. The Bible says the sting of death is sin. Death is the ultimate of all bodily oppression. Jesus, on the cross took care of all that is called sin, once and for all. He was *...bruised for our iniquities: the chastisement of our peace was upon him; and with his stripes we are healed* (Isaiah 53:5). From that day, the price for sin was fully paid.

Now, if sin is the root of sickness and this root has been dealt with, then sickness, the product of sin has been finished. It has no legal right over you any longer. There is no reason sickness should fasten its hold on you now.

Get this right: the man or woman who has a right to divine health is that man or woman who has accepted, believed and acted upon the finished and comprehensive atonement of Christ on the cross.

Anyone, who has not come under the cleansing and atoning blood of Christ cannot be free from sin and its consequences. But if you have done that, you are free from sin, sickness and all satanic wiles. If you can stand on this truth now, the devil himself will acknowledge the fact of it.

We have no legal right to continue in servitude to sin and sickness, because Jesus has really and fully taken our position in these things. We have to believe this before it can be real to us.

Paul said sin shall not have dominion over us. We are no longer under the rulership of the devil because Jesus paid the price. The power that made us free from sin has also made us free from its consequences.

Who hath delivered us from the power

> ***of darkness, and hath translated us into the kingdom of his dear Son:***
>
> *Colossians 1:13*

That you have been delivered from the power of darkness is a fact. It is in the kingdom of darkness that you see and experience everything evil. There, the devil is the king and lord, and he reigns and exercises mastery over every creature under him. He torments them with sickness, poverty and all manner of evil works of darkness. But at new birth, we are delivered from this power of darkness, and translated from that evil kingdom into God's own Kingdom.

The new birth did not leave us at the mercy of the devil. He translated (transferred) us into the Kingdom of light, where darkness cannot approach. Sickness has no place there. It has no power over us anymore. You have been made free, so stay freed.

Remember, sin is the capital source of sickness and it has been dealt with; so, sickness has been taken care of.

Our Redemption from the Curse

The second major source of sickness is the curse of the law. In Deuteronomy 28, from verse 15, the curses of the law are clearly outlined.

> ***If thou wilt not observe to do all the words of this law that are written in this book, that thou mayest fear this glorious and fearful name, THE LORD THY GOD;***
>
> ***Then the LORD will make thy plagues wonderful, and the plagues of thy seed, even great plagues, and of long continuance, and sore sicknesses, and of long continuance.***
>
> ***Moreover he will bring upon thee all the diseases of Egypt, which thou wast afraid of; and they shall cleave unto thee.***
>
> ***Also every sickness, and every plague, which is not written in the book of this law, them will the LORD bring upon thee, until thou be destroyed.***
>
> *Verses 58-61*

You can see from verse 16 to the end of the chapter that the various curses of the law are stated with meticulous clarity.

It is also clear in verses 58-61 that sicknesses and plagues are also covered under the curse of the law. In fact, He went further to say that the sicknesses include those that are not written in this book.

This shows that new sicknesses will come and they have started coming. Just like God is preparing for His end time move, the devil is also doing his worst to mobilise every evil he has in store for his last and final onslaught on humanity. New diseases and sicknesses are coming to light.

Medical science has never gone on recess since its inception. Researches are always going on because something new is always happening, and the devil is playing his last card in a frantic effort to dissuade people from the faith. The truth is that every form of sickness comes under the curse of the law.

Thanks be to God that one of the things Jesus dealt with on the cross is the curse of the law! If He had died by any other means apart from hanging on the cross, the curse of the law would still have been intact, effective and active over us. But the Bible says that Jesus went to the cross to deliver us from that curse. He was there as our substitute. He took our very place under the curse and was cursed for us.

> ***Christ hath redeemed us from the curse of the law, being made a curse for us: for it is written, Cursed is everyone that hangeth on a tree:***
>
> *Galatians 3:13*

The reason Jesus went to the cross was to avert all curses of the law, and sickness is one of them.

Christ has redeemed us from it. He fully bailed us out. Christ has redeemed us from all forms of sickness, disease, and plague including the ones the devil is still planning to introduce to the world. It does not matter what name it is called. You have been made free from it.

For some time now, people have been talking about the deadly AIDS (Acquired Immune Deficiency Syndrome). They have said it is a killer disease and it really is. It is one of the deadliest diseases the devil has ever invented, and medical science has not been able to find an answer to it.

When it strikes a man, it can result into just anything. It is like a sickness machine, it strikes all. It blinds the eyes, paralyses the hands, affects the legs, and even the appetite. It affects all the body system at the same time!

Yet, the devil is planning deadlier ones in times to come. He knows his time is short and has determined to move in an alarming rate. This is why you have to get yourself fully prepared and comprehensively insured against the evil day.

Christ has redeemed us from all these — the curse of the law. He was made a curse for us. If the devil can effectively contest it and argue it out, then we can give up. But the truth is that Jesus really took our place and was made a curse for us. No curse of the law has any legal or illegal right over us any longer.

It is just like Barabbas, the notorious criminal during the earthly walk of the Lord Jesus Christ. The moment he was released in the place of Jesus, no authority in Jerusalem could arrest him anymore. Jesus had taken his place, so he was a free man. Also, Jesus has taken our place under the curse and it covers all forms of sickness, known or unknown. He truly took our place, so we are free.

The way many people respond (instead of reacting against) to sickness, gives the impression that it is God who has put sickness upon them. All they do is complain. They talk, pamper and placate the sickness as if it were from God.

God did not put it there. He does not put sickness on His people. He is the one who has redeemed us from it. If you continue to pose as if God put it there, you will remain under that situation for a long time.

It is time to react against sickness. It is the curse of the law and Christ has redeemed you totally from it.

Satan as the Tormentor

The third source of sickness is satan. It has always been the devil who afflicts people with sickness. In Job 2:7, the Bible records that satan smote Job,

> ***So went Satan forth from the presence of***

the LORD, and smote Job with sore boils from the sole of his foot unto his crown.

Job 2:7

It was satan, not God. Satan was single-handedly responsible for Job's calamities and woes. In the New Testament, Jesus talked of a woman, who had been bound by satan.

And ought not this woman, being a daughter of Abraham, whom Satan hath bound, lo, these eighteen years, be loosed from this bond on the sabbath day?

Luke 13:16

It was satan who bound that woman, not God. Jesus really recognised that satan is in active partnership with sickness. But I have good news for you: the devil is no longer a problem to you. By virtue of the victory of Christ on the cross, you are more than a conqueror over sin, sickness and the devil himself. All you need do is believe these things, and that permanently puts you above the devil.

The Bible says you have the victory in Christ

that overcomes the world, even your faith.

> ***For whatsoever is born of God overcometh the world: and this is the victory that overcometh the world, even our faith.***
>
> *1 John 5:4*

You have world-overcoming faith that wards off all the fiery darts of the devil. He cannot be your problem any longer. You were once under his authority, but you have been transferred from his kingdom into the Kingdom of light. You have been exalted far above him. You are seated together with Christ in the heavenly places far above principalities and powers. You are no longer under him. He is now under your feet (Ephesians 1:20-23, 2:6).

Paul said, *And the God of peace shall bruise Satan (the devil) under your feet shortly...* (Romans 16:20, Paraphrased). That is where he is —under our feet! We were under him, but he is now under our feet.

This is why the Bible commands us not to give place to the devil. In fact, Jesus said we are superior to him. He cannot bring a thing on us because we are his master. Jesus is our

Lord and we are lords to satan and his fallen angels. He cannot force anything on us. He cannot afflict us in anyway. We are far above him in God's order of beings.

It is ridiculous for a messenger to attempt forcing his boss to take orders from him. Likewise, it is above satan to afflict you. Get this fact fully settled in your mind. In it lies your victory.

Whenever he comes against you, resist him. Stand your ground. Refuse to shift an inch and he will definitely flee from you.

> ***...Resist the devil, and he will flee from you.***
>
> *James 4:7*

Friend, you have been set free from these three sources of sickness. Sickness has no power, authority, and right over you. But you need to get acquainted with this fact. Hosea 4:6 says,

> ***My people are destroyed for lack of knowledge...***

You will not be able to act on these facts until you come into the full knowledge; that you have been redeemed and exalted above all these sources of sickness.

3

Stand Your Ground

It is very important for you to know your right and insist on having it. If you do not do this, you may spend a whole lifetime nursing sicknesses and diseases as they come.

I remember many years ago, the devil afflicted me with tuberculosis. I just woke up deep in the night one day and shouted, 'No, no! It is a shame to God that this thing is happening to me. It is a shame to you God! It is a shame!' That was the last I knew of that affliction. It just disappeared and I have been enjoying myself from that time, and I will go on enjoying myself in perfect health! If I did not take my stand, I would still be groaning under that bondage today.

You need to understand very clearly that

you have been redeemed from sickness. There is no reason you should live in it any longer. Christ has done it; therefore, take your stand and get out of that bondage!

John, the beloved apostle, knew this very well. He had the complete redemptive work of Christ in his mind, when he said that God's ultimate and primary desire is for us to prosper and be in health as our souls prosper. In essence, he was saying God's will for us is divine health.

> ***Beloved, I wish above all things that thou mayest prosper and be in health, even as thy soul prospereth.***
>
> *3 John 2*

It is not John wishing here. He is speaking by the inspiration of the Holy Spirit. He is speaking God's mind. The Bible says,

> ***...no prophecy of the scripture is of any private interpretation.***
>
> ***...but holy men of God spake as they were moved by the Holy Ghost.***
>
> 2 Peter 1:20-21

God said, 'My perfect will is for you to be in

health'.

I constantly tell people that God is going to make a clear distinction between His people and the world through health and prosperity.

These are practical things that are obvious to the eyes. Every sick person appreciates health and every poor man knows it is good to be prosperous. Those two areas of life will become the most powerful witnessing tools in the end time.

Your health will be so sound that it will become obvious and unquestionable. The world will know it is real. When a plague afflicts everybody in your compound, you and your family will stand out unaffected. Whatever the plague, written or unwritten, known or unknown; you will stand out as the only person living in health, the plague notwithstanding.

A few years back, the chicken-pox disease took hold of everybody in the compound where I lived. I woke up to see an adult ridiculously painted white. Everybody, except me, was afflicted.

That is the difference. It has to be clear to all that you are extraordinary. This has to be clear to all around you.

There is no precedent in the Word of God for the doctor to say that something is wrong in your body, because Jesus your example and pattern, had nothing wrong in His body.

It does not matter what your state of health was, before you became a believer. The moment you come into the experience of the new birth; God will do all things possible to ensure you are made whole.

A doctor once tested my blood pressure and said, 'Oh, very high!' I said, 'Will you stop that! My blood pressure cannot be high!' I told him, 'Some devil must have entered into your instrument. I am one of the most healthy people on earth. In fact, I am healthier than you. My blood pressure is not high, and cannot be high'. 'If it were not for medical test', I continued, 'I would not have come to you, because I have nothing doing with medical doctors'. Before I walked out of his room, I told him to check himself up, that since he was also touching the instrument as myself, his blood pressure could be the one reading so high!

Now, I have nothing against medical doctors. They are good people, doing their jobs, but I am not their customer.

One of the professions that will be most profitable in this end time is the medical profession. When the plagues begin to attack, people will begin to save for health. People will begin to anticipate sickness. They will begin to easily break down. Almost every unbeliever and ignorant believer will have private doctors. But at such times, we shall be carrying smiling faces all over the place. Then they will know we are different.

I cannot die because of sickness. I have noticed for some time now, each time the enemy sought to attack my body with sickness, I was the one who decided when to be out of it. When I want to be up, a thousand devils cannot hold me down; I get up and that is the end of that sickness. The reason is that I am the one reigning when it comes to that level of life. I determine my health programme.

You have to get to a point where the devil respects you. When it comes to his afflictions over humanity, you are not his equal. You are not on the same level. You are not in the same class of beings. You are superior to him and you are far above him.

Take a diligent look at Deuteronomy 28:15. Look at every curse of the law, one after the other. Then compare those things with what is happening in your life and come out angrily, with a holy wrath and react violently against any trace of the curse in your life.

React against the devil. Ask the enemy this frank question, 'Did Jesus hang on the cross?' He cannot deny it. He will only shiver before you. He knows you have got the key. Tell him that the day Jesus hung on the cross, He was made a curse for you. He took your place and every curse was heaped on Him right there, and you are now free. The devil has no answer to the Word of God, but obedience. That is your freedom.

You need to put more faith in what God says

about you, than in what the doctors say. The doctor says you have an incurable disease and you believe it. Then you begin to plan your funeral before your death; you start to write your will and your handing over note, based on the doctor's report. His report begins to rule your whole system.

The doctor says you have no chance of being pregnant and your heart begins to fail you for fear. He says one of the tubes has been cut off and there is no possibility of pregnancy. That is the doctor's report.

Do not lose sight of the fact that God is not bound to work by human reports. The Bible says you shall know the truth and the truth shall make you free. The Word of God is the truth and the truth shall make you free. The Word of God is truth. Believe God's truth at the expense of the doctor's report and act accordingly.

God is not the author of sickness. He is not in the business of afflicting people with sickness. He is light, and in Him is no darkness at all (1 John 1:5).

> ***Every good gift and every perfect gift is from above, and cometh down from the Father of lights, with whom is no variableness, neither shadow of turning.***
>
> *James 1:17*

He is good altogether. He will be working against Himself if He brings sickness and at the same time heals it; that makes him inconsistent. If He is inconsistent, then He is not God! But thank God, He is the Almighty God. He is not the author of sickness. He does not tempt any man with evil (James 1:13). He is love.

The devil will continue to embarrass and harass you until you violently take your stand against him. He is not a gentleman; so, treat him harshly and violently. The Kingdom of God suffers violence and it is only those that are violent that can take it by force (Matthew 11:12). The Kingdom is taken by a ruthless violence against the devil.

If you pamper and placate disease, it will always make your body a suitable abode.

Before the symptoms begin to manifest, you are already expecting them, and you are already out there looking for sympathisers! This should not be. The Word says, *Neither give place to the devil* (Ephesians 4:27). Also, it is written, ...*Resist the devil, and he will flee from you* (James 4:7).

In addition to all things that the Lord Jesus has done for you, to the detriment of sin, sickness, the curse of the law, and the devil; He has also given you power over all the powers of the devil.

> ***Behold, I give unto you power to tread on serpents and scorpions, and over all the power of the enemy: and nothing shall by any means hurt you.***
>
> *Luke 10:19*

This signifies that in any area, where you and the devil are in conflict, you already have the upper hand. He said, 'I have given you power'. If this is true and you really believe it, you do not have to take it easy with the devil. You need to be ready at all times to react against him in line with the Word of God.

A relation of mine, who is also a doctor, came to my house one day when we had our first baby. He looked at the boy and exclaimed, 'David, your son has jaundice!' 'My son cannot have jaundice!' I declared openly, in the presence of everyone there (they were all intelligent unbelievers). The man who said it himself was an unbeliever. I said, 'My son cannot have jaundice at all!' There was a strong reaction from within me, ready to devour every enemy that might surface.

The Bible says,

> ***For we wrestle not against flesh and blood, but against principalities, against powers...***
>
> *Ephesians 6:12*

You cannot be gentle when you are fighting. My son cannot have jaundice! I just settled it in my spirit.

There was nothing contrary to what I had spoken. I did not even bother to check the boy's eyes. We slept on the same bed, but I did not have time to check! I was fighting. If I checked, I would be giving the devil a point, so

I refused to check.

Sickness has no place in my body and the Bible says my faith sanctifies my son. So, jaundice had no place in him and that settled everything.

Many are too courteous with the devil. This is why they entertain all forms of things in their lives. They are constantly living at the mercy of the devil. But Jesus has finished the work and the price has been fully paid. All you need do is fight your place into it and stand your ground. The faith life is a fight. The Bible says,

> ***Fight the good fight of faith...***
>
> *1 Timothy 6:12*

Sometime ago, death wanted to attack me. Just in a moment, everything changed around me. I could not really understand what was happening. But I suddenly came to some consciousness of the truth about long life. Then I began to say to myself, 'I am superior to this situation; I am above this!' As I said this, the Master spoke quietly to me, 'If you are above this, then stand up'.

Those on-the-bed confessions cannot bring you to a place of health. You will have to stand, get out of bed, dress up and go out! If you are alright, you have no business staying there.

You may have listened to many messages about healing and health. You may have even read many books on that subject, but until you become a fighter and really fight your way into it, you will not get it. It does not matter what has been done on you. What the doctor says is not important. The important thing is that God's will for you is health.

Abraham was strong and still ran freely at age 90. At 120 years, Moses was still very strong! The Bible says his natural strength was not abated neither did his eyes grow dim (Deuteronomy 34:7). That is divine health.

If at your present age, you patronise chemists and pharmaceutical stores, what will you look like when you are 80? If you really understand divine health, you will respond to it from within.

Paul was one man whom the devil knew and respected. He said, *Jesus I know, and Paul I know.* Paul was a no-nonsense preacher, a touch-me-not preacher, and a fire brand. He was described as a 'pestilent fellow' in Acts 24:5. He had to command blindness on Elymas, so the devil knew and respected him. He was one person, who did not give the devil any place. Do not give place to the devil.

Do not treat any bodily ailment as ordinary. React against it, as you will react against the worst plague in the world today. There was a time I had to preach and shortly before I got to the auditorium, the devil wanted to attack me with running nose. I reacted violently against it. I said, 'No, it is impossible for me to preach with running nose. Jesus has paid for it and I am free!' I then threw my handkerchief away, so that I could not have a way of helping it. That moment, all the fluid in my nostrils dried up.

Many believers are too decent and courteous for a miracle. Get out of your shell and get your miracle!

There was a woman, a former neighbour, whose child had an inexplicable disease. The child's stomach kept swelling. The stomach was so swollen that it began to shine. You cannot call that stomach ache because it was more than that. It was the devil in action. It came to a point that the woman was on the verge of frustration, she helplessly watched her child dying.

She then ran, almost uncovered to my apartment and reported that her child was dying. I just took my time to get there. The child was staring into space. He could not blink his eyes any more. A kind of grief got hold of me from within. I just hated the devil.

This is the type of grief you need. Such situations deserve an inner reaction —a grief. You know the Bible says Jesus was grieved in the spirit. The moment I saw the child, I got hold of him, pressed his stomach against my body and said, 'Come on, satan, loose your hold over this child'.

Immediately, the whole place was in a mess, as all the rubbish the devil had loaded in the child's belly was flushed out and he was made whole. If all I did was to plead and be gentlemanly about it, nothing would have happened to the child's advantage. The devil would have killed him! The Kingdom of God suffers violence, and it is only those that are violent that can take it by force!

There are many people that have been praying about certain things for a long time, but have not got it. Quite a number of the things you have been praying to God for do not need prayers. All you need is to go and take them. If you continue in your prayers, they may not really come; but when you get stirred up within you, and you march forward and lay hold on them, nobody can stop you. They are yours, credited to your account.

God's declared will is 3 John 2. His desire for you is to prosper and be in health as your soul prospers. He said you should go and be sick no more. Jesus is our perfect example. If you are sick, you are taking after yourself, not Jesus. He was never sick and you do not have any reason to be sick. He wants you to live all your days in perfect health!

Do not forget that one basic step to victorious living over sickness is the new birth. If you have not experienced that, now is the time.

You need to insure your life in God; then you will be able to enjoy your right to divine health.

4

God's Master Key To Divine Health

It is very important for us to live in the consciousness of the truth that, among other things, Jesus has taken away our sicknesses. If we know how expensive it is to keep a healthy body in the world today, we will give praise to God for the health we enjoy now because we are in His service. He said if we serve Him, He will remove sickness from us (Exodus 23:25).

One of the areas the devil will really publicise himself in this end time, is in the area of sickness. On the other hand, God is going to strongly establish His covenant of divine health with His people.

Through divine health, God is going to make the difference clear between His people and the rest of the world. God has contracted a covenant of good health with His people from the beginning. He has spoken to our fathers, Abraham, Isaac and Jacob. Sickness was strange to them. They did not have any reason to be sick. The covenant forbade them to be sick.

> ***My covenant will I not break, nor alter the thing that is gone out of my lips.***
>
> *Psalm 89:34*

They were under a great covenant. We have been brought under this same covenant also by the death and resurrection of the Lord Jesus Christ.

> ***Christ hath redeemed us from the curse of the law, being made a curse for us: for it is written, Cursed is everyone that hangeth on a tree:***
>
> ***That the blessing of Abraham might come on the Gentiles through Jesus Christ; that we might receive the promise of the Spirit through faith.***
>
> *Galatians 3:13-14*

Christ came to make us partakers of this great covenant of divine health. The covenant belongs to us also. However, there are some things you need to do. If you leave them undone, your health is not guaranteed. You need to do them and observe them closely to be in health.

God has paid for every inconvenience within and outside us. He has no plan for any part of our bodies to harbour any form of pain. But it takes doing what God has said, to stay in that high premise of divine health.

Take a look at Isaiah 33:5-6, and you will find a few things there,

> ***The LORD is exalted; for he dwelleth on high: He hath filled Zion with judgment and righteousness.***
>
> ***And wisdom and knowledge shall be the stability of thy times, and strength of salvation: the fear of the LORD is his treasure.***

Look at verse 6 again. It says, *And wisdom and knowledge shall be the stability of thy times....* Wisdom is the accurate application of knowledge.

Jesus said,

> ***And ye shall know the truth, and the truth shall make you free.***
>
> *John 8:32*

The point being made here is that the stability of our times comes by the accurate application of the knowledge of the truth which we possess. The amount of wisdom we put in determines how stable our times will be.

God is exalted on high, no doubt. He has filled Zion with judgment and with righteousness; it is now Zion's responsibility to seek wisdom and knowledge for stability. God spoke a lot of things about knowledge in the scriptures. Knowledge is absolutely indispensable, if you are to walk with God.

> ***Grace and peace be multiplied unto you through the knowledge of God, and of Jesus our Lord,***
>
> ***According as his divine power hath given unto us all things that pertain unto life and godliness, through the knowledge of him that hath called us to glory and virtue:***
>
> *2 Peter 1:2-3*

He has given us all things that pertain to life and godliness, but they are only available through the knowledge of Him. The things He has made available are only workable, if they are known and applied. True, He has given us all things, but we may not get one per cent of it in this world if we do not know that they have been made available to us.

God has not called us to suffering and sickness. He has called us to glory and virtue. If sickness is glorious and virtuous, then it is possible God has called us into it; but there is no glory in sickness. There is no virtue in disease! God has given us all that makes for life and godliness.

There are quite a number of people today who are under the devil in secret cults. They are afraid of life and they want security. Only very few of them are there for money. Majority of them are wealthy. They are not looking for money. What they want is guaranteed long life and health. But the Bible says that in this process, they are under a lifetime of bondage.

However, this long life is freely available in

Christ. You do not need to drink human blood to be secure. It is freely given in Christ. If you want your life to be preserved, join the Jesus people, the company of light.

All things that make for life and godliness have been made available to you, but they will not be released without knowledge. God has not called you to shame or evil; He has called you unto glory and virtue.

Sickness is not glorious; health is glorious. It is what you can talk proudly about. You can say it to everybody. You can say, 'I can do all things through Christ who strengthens me'. That will only come when you become conscious of these things, and God's divine health will be at work within you.

> ***Whereby are given unto us exceeding great and precious promises: that by these ye might be partakers of the divine nature, having escaped the corruption that is in the world through lust.***
>
> *2 Peter 1:4*

Most definitely, sickness is one of the corrupting weapons in the world today. If sickness strikes a man, you will suddenly notice that the man begins to deteriorate in strength and form. In no time, you notice that he now has sunken cheeks and a gloomy face. He becomes miserable. That is the corrupting influence of sickness. But you have become a partaker of the divine nature and so have escaped this corruption.

This divine nature is void of sickness. Jesus operated in it and sickness could not attack Him. The essence of the Scriptures is to make you become a partaker of this divine nature and by the knowledge of it, you enter into divine health. It is not automatic. You do not enjoy it, until you have come into a full knowledge of it and it is rightly applied. It does not jump on people; it answers to a full appraisal and application of the scriptures concerning it.

Divine Health is a covenant issue, and every covenant has two sides to it. God can never deny Himself. When you fulfil your own part, God has no choice but to fulfil His own.

If you are going to truly partake of the divine nature, it has to be through the knowledge of Him who has called you to glory and virtue. This knowledge is the knowledge of the exceeding great and precious promises. This very knowledge, clearly understood and accurately applied, will cause you to escape the corruption of sickness.

This truth is important to your life, because you are either in the mainstream of God's move or you are out of it. If you do not take your own place in divine health, by the time people are enjoying and walking in it, you will be asking and looking for reasons yours is not coming forth.

There is a way to divine health and this is the secret. God does not intend to keep anything from us. The Bible says, unto us that believe it is given to know the mysteries of the Kingdom (Matthew 13:11). It is good for you to know that the mystery of divine health is yours by right of covenant relationship.

It is your knowledge of the Word that will produce your being like Jesus, in any area of life where you want to be like Him. When you have the revealed Word in any area, it becomes easy for you to operate adequately to the fulfilment of the Scriptures on that subject. It is the same with divine health.

> ***Bless the LORD, O my soul, and forget not all his benefits:***
>
> ***Who forgiveth all thine iniquities; who healeth all thy diseases;***
>
> ***Who redeemeth thy life from destruction; who crowneth thee with lovingkindness and tender mercies;***
>
> ***Who satisfieth thy mouth with good things; so that thy youth is renewed like the eagle's.***
>
> *Psalm 103:2-5*

Jesus came for the whole man - spirit, soul and body. He wants every part of us to reflect His glory. His mission does not stop with sin. He came that you might have life, and have it more abundantly.

The Church has been held in this ugly situation for too long. People have always believed that God is only interested in saving sinners. That is why sickness invaded the Church and every Church has prayer for the sick on its prayer list. But now that the word of health is coming to light in the body, things are changing.

Sickness now fears the body of Christ and it will yet fear us the more. It is the same in the area of prosperity. I have seen Church buildings built over a period of 20 years, yet to be completed. They still carry blocks and planks all over the place. But the time is at hand, when these things will change totally and it has started.

When you come to the understanding that there are more benefits in Christ than escaping into heaven, you will begin to enjoy them. It says not to forget His *benefits* (that is plural). The benefits are many.

One of the benefits is that He renews your youth as the eagle's. When you are 50 years, you are still operating as a youngster. At 60, you are still operating as if you are 25. At 80, your physique is still sound and good to look at. When you are 99 years, you are still running like Abraham. These are all benefits of Christ's coming.

5

God's Medicine

God's Word is His medicine for the believer. Many people wonder what keeps us going without patronising the clinics and chemists. We have our own brand of medicine that is more effective than medical science. It is God's Word!

> ***My son, attend to my words; incline thine ear unto my sayings.***
>
> ***Let them not depart from thine eyes; keep them in the midst of thine heart.***
>
> ***For they are life unto those that find them, and health to all their flesh.***
>
> *Proverbs 4:20-22*

The Word is health to all their flesh — healthy livers, kidneys, intestines, bones, marrows, eyes, ears, nose, mouths, and legs. It is health to every part of the body of whosoever finds it. The moment the Word enters into you, you become a different person altogether. The Word transforms your body to health.

God's Word is an all-purpose drug. Actually, the word translated 'health' in verse 22 is also translated 'medicine'. It is an all-purpose medicine sent to us by God, to immunise us against all forms of sickness and to keep us healthy all the time. All we need do now is find out how to administer God's medicine in our own situation. This is where wisdom comes in.

Wisdom and knowledge shall be the stability of our times (Isaiah 33:6). In the physical, if a doctor gives you some drugs, he will definitely give you the prescription for maximum results. If you are given injection to be injected directly into the blood streams, and you decided to use your discretion and mix it with your food as a time-saving device (after all, it will get into the body at last), you will run into difficulties.

In the same way, if you are given drugs and asked to take a specific number of tablets at a specific time for effect, perhaps two in the morning, two in the afternoon and two in the evening; you cannot say, 'Well, thank God, I will not be able to wait for this long. As a matter of fact, I will be away for the next two weeks' and then you take the six doses all at once in the morning. You will endanger yourself, and that may cost you your life!

You have got the right drugs, but you have not used them appropriately. On the same note, you cannot expect to have the best results by reducing the specified dosage.

God's Word is medicine. It is drug (health) to your body —every part of your body.

A friend of mine (a man of God) used to be a stammerer. He could not speak well. But the Word got into him and knocked out every bit of stammering. He is now a fluent and eloquent speaker, one of the best the world has ever known. He is a man of great speech! The Word did it.

I have been with him in many private and open discussions, and there is no trace of stammering in him. When the Word enters a man, it transforms him completely.

One of my cousins came and said, 'Uncle, I have some problem with my eyes'. I gave Him God's medicine and it worked for him. 'It is health to all their flesh'.

When the Lord brought this revelation into my consciousness, it knocked all odd ways of praying for the sick out of me. It used to be 'Lord, heal him if it be Thy will, but heavenly Father, grant them strength to bear it so that they can see Thy glory'. What glory is in sickness? It was a common thing for them to be sick. They all bragged about their ability to endure sickness.

But the Bible says, the Word is medicine to all your flesh.

> ***For the word of God is quick, and powerful, and sharper than any twoedged sword, piercing even to the dividing asunder of soul and spirit, and of the joints and marrow, and is a discerner of the thoughts and intents of the heart.***
>
> *Hebrews 4:12*

The Word is quick: living and powerful. It

can combat any form of sickness and win. It is powerfully alive. It is capable of healing all manner of sickness. It penetrates into the spirit and the soul. It gets into your entire system and works effectually there. It carries out operations in your bones and marrows. You do not need all those painful processes in the medical theatre. All you need is God's medicine, the all-purpose drug. It will make you whole.

When the doctor recommends amputation because rheumatism has eaten into your marrows, you will need to apply God's medicine. The Bible says the Word penetrates into the joints and marrows. Medical science believes blood is manufactured in the marrow. Thank God the Word gets there! That is why it is health and medicine to all our flesh. When the Word enters you, it sharpens you out and makes you look like God here on earth.

There is a great healing effect in the Word of God. If anybody says something is wrong with your system, tell that person you know the answer. It is the Word.

The man of God, Dr Kenneth Hagin, was holding a meeting in a Church and ministering to the sick. However, the Pastor of this church did not believe in divine healing. But Dr Hagin continued to minister, and the sick started getting healed. It came to a point that he became tired and there was a woman, who was brought in on a wheel chair. She had been in that state for a long time. The church Pastor quickly went to Kenneth Hagin, giving him the case history of the sickness. He said the woman had not walked for nine years, and doctors said she would never walk again in her life. He tried to convince Kenneth Hagin against praying for her.

But despite the fact that he was tired, Kenneth Hagin said the Word is never tired, and went ahead to minister to this woman. He opened 1 Peter 2:24 and placed it on the woman's laps.

> ***Who his own self bare our sins in his own body on the tree, that we, being dead to sins, should live in righteousness: BY WHOSE STRIPES YE WERE HEALED.***
>
> *(Emphasis Mine)*

He asked her, 'Is '**were**' present, past or future tense?' The woman said, 'past'. He said to her, 'That means you have been healed before now!' The woman was amazed and wondered where such scripture had been all these years. He asked her to begin to thank God for her healing and urged the congregation to join her in praising the Lord. She was still on the chair, but the Word says she had been healed. Ten minutes later, she was out of the wheel chair, very sound, never to sit in there again!

While she was thanking God, the Word was carrying out all operations in her system, replacing dead tissues and supplying new sets of bones. It penetrated into every area that needed attention and got the woman on her feet again, contrary to the doctor's report and certification.

The Word made the difference. That Word will make the difference in you too! It is not the one you have in your head; it is the Word in your heart. *Keep them in the midst of thine heart* (Proverbs 4:21).

Your heart is the only good ground where

the Word can grow and produce fruit. When it enters into you, it will make all the difference, and heal every part of your body. Your whole system will receive adequate attention from the Word, the moment it enters into your heart. When I got this Word, I said, 'This is what everybody should be told. It is not just to increase their scriptural vocabulary'.

There are many people today, who can quote series of scriptures, but have never drawn any benefit from them. They know it, but it does not profit them. It has not entered their hearts. They need just more than being able to quote it. The Bible talks of some people who heard the Word, but did not benefit from it. You need to know how to apply the Word based on Proverbs 4:20. He said, 'My son, attend to my words!' God intends you to create time for His Word. Be available to the Word. Wait on the Word. We talk very much about waiting on the Lord, but have done very little of waiting on the Word. But He said here that we should wait on the Word.

That is God's prescription. The devil knows that any Word that enters us makes us his master in that area. When the Word of holiness enters us, it makes us masters over sin. Same with prosperity and divine health. This is why we have to attend to the Word. It is our live-wire, it determines our life content and quality.

The second prescription is 'incline thine ear unto my sayings'. Be totally attentive to the Spirit. Somebody once asked me if I memorise scriptures. No, I do not. When it enters into you, it becomes part of you— just like your name.

You do not need to memorise your name, you know it and respond to it instinctively. If the Word should enter into you, it would require your attention —give ear to it. If faith for divine health has to enter into you, you must give ear to it.

> ***So then faith cometh by hearing, and hearing by the word of God.***
>
> *Romans 10:17*

It is hearing the Word that transformed Reverend Kenneth Copeland's life. Give ear to the Word. Hear it preached. Take time to be attentive. Many people hear the Word with a careless approach. Jesus said, 'Take heed how ye hear'. Hear the Word with seriousness of mind. This is important.

I taught at a seminar on divine healing in February 1984. One of the men in attendance had been under severe oppression of the devil. He had been passing out blood for many years. In fact, he could be rightly called 'the man with the issue of blood'. He had tried every possible means to be healed, but nothing happened.

He was finally booked for an operation. However, he was at this seminar and heard the Word on divine healing. He received the Word, it entered and began a surgical operation in his body.

As the seminar progressed, he felt a pulling force in his system. At that instance, he went to the toilet to ease himself. To his surprise, the issue of blood ceased and he became a normal person. There was no need for the operation any more. The Word had done it; pain-free! From that day, the man made it a point of duty to attend all our meetings. That is the effect the Word will produce, if you will give ear to it diligently.

You do not need all the pains medical science entails to get your healing and be in health. All you need is to attend to the Word, and give ear to it. Hearing the Word helped this man. He could have died during the operation that was barely days ahead. But the Word, God's medicine made all the difference between life and death for him.

As you give ear to the Word, it will produce the same results in you also! There is no limit to what the Word will produce in you. I have seen women give birth without labour. This is contrary to medical science. But thank God, we are not medical people, we are supernatural people! The Bible says, ... *she shall be saved in childbearing, if they continue in faith and charity and holiness...* (1 Timothy 2:15). That means that as long as they continue hearing to produce faith, they will be saved during childbearing. The moment this Word enters you and gets hold of you, you become a master in childbearing. It is not more than going to toilet any more.

Remember these two major keys: one, to attend to the Word; create time for it if you want divine healing virtue to be released into your system. Two, give ear to the Word, by listening to messages on CD, DVD and other available channel, reading the Bible and anointed books; be wholeheartedly attentive to it. That is the secret of victorious living.

The next step is: 'Let them not depart from thine eyes'. There is health virtue in looking. Keep your eyes glued to the Word.

There was a time judgment came into the camp of Israel in the wilderness. They were bitten in their thousands by fiery serpents. Moses, the man of God prayed and God asked him to make a fiery serpent of brass and hang it up on a tree so that any man who took time to look upon the serpent might be saved. Moses did this, and everyone who looked upon the brazen serpent was saved from the fiery serpents.

And Moses made a serpent of brass, and put it upon a pole, and it came to

pass, that if a serpent had bitten any man, when he beheld (looked at) the serpent of brass, he lived.

Numbers 21:9 (Paraphrased)

You have to keep looking at the Word. When situations come against you, do not focus on them; focus on what God has said about you. Hebrews 12:2 says,

Looking unto Jesus the author and finisher of your faith...

In John 3:14, Jesus is likened to that fiery serpent of brass. If the serpent of brass could bring health, looking unto Jesus will bring greater (divine) health. The psalmist knew the secret of looking. The people of old looked unto the Word and they were not ashamed. As long as you keep the Word in sight, it will produce the desired results.

They looked unto him, and were lightened: and their faces were not ashamed.

Psalm 34:5

That is the effect of looking unto Jesus.

> ***But we all, with open face beholding as in a glass the glory of the Lord, are changed into the same image from glory to glory, even as by the Spirit of the Lord.***
>
> *2 Corinthians 3:18*

The glass referred to here is the Word of God, according to James 1:23-25. The glass is the perfect law of liberty — the Word of God. Keep looking at it until it transforms you from the body of sickness to the body of divine health. There is power in the Word; it will move you from the natural into the supernatural, from the ordinary into the extraordinary and from yourself into God Himself. It will bring you into the same level of bodily glory with the Lord.

If we want our health to be like the health of Jesus, we have to keep looking unto Him, by looking up at everything He has said about us in His Word. We must take time to look at His exceeding great and precious promises. As we focus on them, they will rise within us and devour every form of sickness and produce bodies of health in us.

One important thing to note is that you do not need to look at or attend to symptoms. He said, 'Attend to My words!' You have nothing to worry about when you attend to His Word. When you notice that certain symptoms are trying to show up in your system, you look at the Word — Surely, He hath borne my sicknesses upon His own body and by His stripes I was healed.

There are many things that will want to demand your attention, but refuse them. Attend to the Word only, and your victory is as sure as ever. These are basic spiritual laws. If you apply them correctly, you will get the results. No one has ever been disappointed after applying the Word appropriately. It is a basic fact. The Word carries God's life, and His integrity backs His Word up. It cannot fail.

If the Word says, 'Look', all you need do is look. Forget about every other thing around you and concentrate on what God has said. Look at the case of the people of Israel. As many as looked got saved. But all those who died were the ones who felt that looking would not do any good. The secret is in simple obedience to the Word. Close your eyes and ears to everything and focus on the Word. It will do you good in times of trouble.

The psalmist said, *I will lift up mine eyes unto the hills, from whence cometh my help.* He knew all the troubles were here below, but he refused to focus on the problems. He focused on the source of solution. That is the whole idea about looking unto Jesus, the author and finisher of our faith.

Wisdom and knowledge shall be the stability of our times. Knowing what God has said and knowing how to apply it will make a diligent and stable fighter out of you and you will find life very exciting.

6

Apply The Word

The Lord is more eager to set you free from your afflictions than you are ready to be freed. This is why Jesus came. God sent Him into the world to save, heal, and deliver.

The devil had held mankind in a terrible and oppressive reign. So, God sent Jesus Christ into the world, that He might destroy all the works of the devil. His major assignment was to undo all that the enemy had done and to restore all that he had stolen from mankind. He came and fulfilled this mission comprehensively.

> ***He that committeth sin is of the devil; for the devil sinneth from the beginning. For this purpose the Son of God was manifested, that he might***

> ***destroy the works of the devil.***
>
> *1 John 3:8*

Sin is just one of the many works of the devil. He is the originator of sickness and responsible for every disease. Hence, Jesus came to destroy his works. That is why He came! He came to loose those that are bound, and to wipe away all tears. He came to do a total overhauling of mankind.

> ***How God anointed Jesus of Nazareth with the Holy Ghost and with power: who went about doing good, and healing all that were oppressed of the devil; for God was with him.***
>
> *Acts 10:38*

All bodily ailments and afflictions are oppressions of the devil. So, God sent Jesus and anointed Him to set them loose, and to destroy the devil's works. It is important for you to know that His ministry has not changed. He is still healing the sick and destroying the works of the devil today! He is the same yesterday, today, and forever (Hebrews 13:8).

If He cleansed lepers, He is still cleansing them today. If He healed the blind, He will still do it today. Anything He did that time; He will still do today. He is the unchanging One. It was for this reason that He came: to destroy and wipe out all the works of the enemy.

God does not intend for us to be in bondage to the devil. He has no plan for that at all. He has made all provisions for our being in health. He sent Jesus to ensure that we are in health.

Many people believe that God is training them through hardship. No! He is not. Jesus has passed through that for us. We do not need the hardship anymore; sickness has no power over us. We have been redeemed from it. The Bible says we have been bought with a price, so we must glorify God in our spirits, souls and bodies which are God's.

Your body must be a testimony of health to the world. A sick body cannot be a testimony of God's glory. You must know that nothing should happen to you, except all that is written about you. Nothing happened to the Lord Jesus

Christ, apart from what was written about Him. The Bible says you will serve the Lord your God and He will remove sickness from you. He said nothing shall cast your young.

Miscarriage is not written about you! Everything may be contrary to what you see in the Word, but *...faith is the substance of things hoped for, the evidence of things not seen* (Hebrews 11:1).

It is what you say about the situation around you that happens to you. Speak the things that are written of you and they will become real to you. The Word cannot fail; therefore, stand on it and it will prevail over all circumstances. Faith is seeing the invisible. Everything you can see around is physical.

> ***While we look not at the things which are seen, but at the things which are not seen: for the things which are seen are temporal; but the things which are not seen are eternal.***
>
> *2 Corinthians 4:18*

The Bible says the flesh profits nothing, but the Spirit quickens. The visible (physical) profits nothing. It is the Spirit (invisible) that is profitable for faith.

Understand this very clearly that you determine what happens to you. Jesus has paid the price. God has spoken well about you. The only thing to do is to put faith in all these and you are in health.

I would like to draw your attention, in this chapter to how you can enjoy your health over internal problems. It does not matter what problem it is. Jesus came to destroy all the works of the devil, and that includes internal problems. As you allow the Word to enter into you, miracles will happen and you will walk out free.

Note that every disorder inside your body is the work of the devil. God made everything perfect in you; He did not make any mistake. If there is a wrong thing in you, it is the devil's work and Jesus came to abolish them all.

In the preceding chapter, we saw three basic steps in applying the Word of God:

- Attend to the Word
- Give ear to His sayings, and
- Let them not depart from your eyes.

These are very important steps. If you have to get results from the Word, it must be applied as prescribed. God's prescription is 'Attend to My words, give ear to My sayings, and let them not depart from thine eyes'. It states further, 'Keep them in the midst of thine heart', make it your thought.

Let it be the only thing you are thinking about. Let your whole thought be anchored on God's Word, not on your doctor's word. The Bible says whatever you think in your heart rules your entire being. *For as he thinketh in his heart, so is he…* (Proverbs 23:7).

If your heart is fully settled and established on what God has said about your body, it will obviously respond accordingly. Your heart is the seat of your miracle. It is what comes out of your heart that rules your life.

> ***Keep thy heart with all diligence; for out of it are the issues of life.***
>
> *Proverbs 4:23*

What you think matters much to your quality of life. If you think sickness, you will get sickness. If you think poverty, you will get it. If it is health you think, you will be healthy. It is important for you to take note of what you think. Your heart is the miracle spot. If your heart says there is no miracle, you cannot get one.

> ***... for out of the abundance of the heart the mouth speaketh.***
>
> *Matthew 12:34*

You actually determine what happens to you from the heart. It is from there you bring forth good treasures and bring forth evil. God is more particular about what we think.He understands the thoughts of man. He knows what we think. He wants the Word to become the focus on our thoughts. Use it in your thinking.

Until you begin to allow the Word to penetrate your thinking faculty, your miracle will take time to come. Shift your thoughts from situations, circumstances, symptoms and feelings. Concentrate on whatever God says about your health. That is the secret.

When it comes to a warfare on your health, allow Matthew 8:17 to take hold of your thought, He said, *...Himself took our infirmities, and bare our sicknesses*. Matthew quoted from the Messianic prophecy in Isaiah 53. It is talking about Jesus having taken our infirmities and sicknesses. Anchor your thought on that, and allow it to monitor your thinking. By this, your health will spring forth with beauty every day.

Jesus said whosoever shall say with his mouth and not doubt in his heart will have whatsoever he says (Mark 11:23). It means the performance of the things said depends on the state of the heart. If your heart is not established in the Word, you cannot have what you are saying.

Peter the apostle robbed himself of the privilege of successfully walking on water with Jesus because he shifted his thought to the possibility of drowning when he saw the storm and the billows. He took his eyes off the Master, and that was how far he could go.

Many people have robbed themselves of God's blessings, by entertaining dangerous thoughts. Your thoughts play a key role in your life. You cannot grow beyond your thought life. *As a man thinketh in his heart, so is he.* Think on the Word, it will produce life in your body and you will live in good health.

In the parable of the sower, Jesus said the heart of man is the good ground. That is where the Word will grow and bear fruit. It is not your head.

There are many things going on in some people's lives, because they have the Word in their heads and not their hearts. Keep it in your heart. With the heart man believes, not with the head. Faith is of the heart. It is not the things you say, but what you believe in your heart, and say with your mouth!

Think health and live long, think strength and be strong, think prosperity and prosper; think protection and live in God's eternal security. God does not plan that you should think negative. He has given you enough to think about. He has allocated all your time to thinking in the Word of God. In Joshua, He said (think) meditate upon it, day and night—all the time.

People are defeated because they think on other things apart from the Word. They get caught up in thinking the problem. When anything is about to happen, they are already lost in thought about the possible consequences, instead of thinking on what God has said about such situations. People say, 'Pastor, you do not understand my situation. My own experience is peculiar'. How peculiar? God says think on things that are of good report. The solution God has given about the problem is the good report you should think on.

> ***Finally, brethren, whatsoever things are true, whatsoever things are honest, whatsoever things are just, whatsoever things are pure, whatsoever things are lovely, whatsoever things are of good report; if there be any virtue, and if there be any praise, think on these things.***
>
> *Philippians 4:8*

Are you looking for things to think about? They are clearly stated in Philippians 4:8. If you keep thinking the problems, you will find it very difficult and even impossible to get out of them.

You need to take Jesus as your personal physician. The Bible says, 'I am the Lord that healeth thee'. He is saying, 'I am your personal physician'. If you take Him as your personal physician with the same seriousness with which you take Him as your Saviour, you will stay healthy always.

He will not take anything from you. He does not need those things that doctors request for. He will only give you a good time and tell you, 'Be of good courage, your problems are over'. That is why He came.

In my student days, I was in a situation which would take only a miracle to solve. I made up my mind to get the miracle—I wanted to pass an examination I did not write! The devil came (not as the devil) to offer some 'nice' religious advice. He actually wanted me to be double-minded, and of course, a double-minded person cannot receive a miracle!

The Bible talks of the devil going about like a roaring lion, looking for whom he may devour

(1 Peter 5:8). But I resisted him and got my miracle. A double-minded man is unstable in all his ways.

The moment the thought came, I took my stand before God and all living beings in heaven, and refused to be moved. If you are going to get your miracle, determine to be single minded about it. Do not shift your ground, no matter how little. It should not even cross your mind. Be bold about it.

I have come to know that one of the ways the enemy deceives God's people into missing their blessings of health is through procrastination. They keep saying if it does not happen today, it will happen in the next service. If it does not come this year, it will come next year. Why is it not possible now? God is always ready. He is eager to do it; you are the only problem.

Stop being double-minded about it and lay hold on your blessings. The point is that you need to keep your heart with all diligence. That is the best way you can keep away from being double-minded.

Get the understanding that many times, your problem is not that God has not heard you. It is simply that you have allowed yourself to waver in heart and your blessing is hanging out there in the heavenlies. You cannot get it that way; a double-minded person cannot receive anything from God. You have no reason or basis to be double-minded.

You have the Bible. The Holy Ghost is in you. You know how to pray and that God must answer you, when you pray aright. Your miracle is meant for the now, not later. Learn to force this down the devil's throat. Let him know you know what you are doing. Tell him your miracle of health is now. The moment you make up your mind, no devil can stop your miracle. You just know that you have it right there.

God is not procrastinating on your case. He sends your miracle with dispatch. He is very eager. He keeps deploying, redeploying and mobilising the angels on your behalf.

God is the end of all our troubles. Many people are yet to know that if one believes with the heart, one must speak it in boldness.

Some believers speak things that are contrary to their faith. They claim to have faith, but the things they speak are a departure from what they believe. This is another hindrance to your miracle.

> ***Put away from thee a froward mouth, and perverse lips put far from thee.***
>
> *Proverbs 4:24*

Keep talking the truth. Confess the truth of the Word of God about the situation. That is the summary of that verse. It is not enough to believe; your confession has to be in line with what you believe. What you say is very important to the ultimate realisation of your miracle. The power of life and death lies in your mouth.

> ***Death and life are in the power of the tongue: and they that love it shall eat the fruit thereof.***
>
> *Proverbs 18:21*

After you have believed, do not allow any negative statement from your lips; so, stand against it consciously. The power that will liberate your health is in your tongue. If you believe in health, you have to say it loud with your mouth. It is a spiritual law that cannot be broken. With the heart man believes and with the mouth confession is made. Say it!

> ***We having the same spirit of faith, according as it is written, I believed, and therefore have I spoken; we also believe, and therefore speak.***
>
> *2 Corinthians 4:13*

When you believe, you have to speak it out with boldness. Your faith must find expression in words. The Word you believe in your heart, formed by the mouth and released in words is a creative force. It is as powerful and effective as God speaking it. The Bible says in Hebrews 11:3,

> ***Through faith we understand that the worlds were framed by the word of God...***

God spoke and the worlds came into being. Jesus said we should also possess the faith of God. God's kind of faith is the faith that is expressed in words. It makes great creative power available. By expressing our faith in words, we become co-creators with God. That is what God expects of us.

When a man who has been diagnosed as having cancer, has a basis in the Word of God in Matthew 8:17; 1 Peter 2:24; Exodus 23:25-26 and Isaiah 53:5, to say, 'I do not have cancer, Jesus has taken my disease and sickness away; I am made whole spirit, soul and body', he gets his deliverance from cancer. Such is the power of words spoken in faith. It has no limit. It is divine wisdom.

God has never done anything without saying it. He has designed the same way of getting victory for us. Whatever sickness may have plagued your life and however long it has been, the moment you begin to release words based on the word of health, something positive begins to happen to you and your results will surely come.

Therefore, put away every negative and perverse speech from you. Do not speak evil, the words that you speak rule your life. You will get the things you speak in faith. Life and death are in the power of the tongue.

When people want to know how you feel,

say, 'I am fine, strong, energetic and very fit for the day!' Refuse to say any perverse thing about yourself. If you must stay in health, you must learn to speak choice words, seasoned with salt, to minister grace, strength and health to your body and to them that hear you.

When I was in school, an unbeliever came asking me about the examination we had just written. I said that the paper was the cheapest I had ever written. Everybody was dazed. They had all been complaining about the paper. But I knew the Bible says I should put away every froward speech and perverse tongue. They said nobody might pass the paper, but I said, 'If all of you fail, I will be the only one who will pass'. I knew I should be careful what I say. I said the right words. I said it boldly that I would pass. I am not a failure. I am an embodiment of success. That is the truth.

You also will need to learn to take your stand. Do not compromise it. Unbelievers will come to respect you, as you speak the Word of God from your lips in faith. Your victory will come through the power-loaded words that proceed from your mouth.

The Bible says the Word is sharper than any two-edged sword. When you speak the Word in faith, you are releasing some powerful weapons of war.

Jesus did not speak anything contrary to the Word. He was constantly fighting the devil. It ought to be the same with you. Release them against the devil.

Right words are powerful. They are power containers. Nothing can stand against them. No symptom can stand against them because they are forceful.

> ***How forcible are right words...***
>
> *Job 6:25*

Stop using words carelessly. Much importance is attached to your words. Speak right words and you will get right results.

God is releasing you into a realm of liberty and health right now. Only stand in the truth and apply the Word rightly. Your mere obedience to this Word will determine a lot of things in your life. It will open doors of victory in all areas of your life.

7

Follow the Steps of The Fathers

By now, you have come to a positive and definite knowledge of God's will for your divine health. It is your sonship right. The Bible tells us we are Abraham's seed. So, we should do the deeds of Abraham. If Abraham is our father and we are his seeds, we must identify with Abraham's works. Abraham was a man of faith. He is best known as the father of faith. He was busy doing faith.

Looking at the Word of God, we discovered that if we must get Abraham's result, we must do what he did. He was a man who depended solely on the Word God gave him. He did not consider the situation around him. He hoped against hope! When things were obviously negative, he chose to believe what God had said about him, the situation notwithstanding. That is the picture of a man who would go places with God. The only evidence he had was the Word God gave him.

> ***...but to that also which is of the faith of Abraham; who is the father of us all,***
>
> ***Who against hope believed in hope, that he might become the father of many nations; according to that which was spoken, So shall thy seed be.***
>
> ***And being not weak in faith, he considered not his own body now dead, when he was about an hundred years old, neither yet the deadness of Sara's womb:***
>
> ***He staggered not at the promise of God through unbelief; but was strong in faith, giving glory to God;***
>
> ***And being fully persuaded that, what he had promised, he was able also to perform.***
>
> *Romans 4:16, 18-21*

That tells the story of Abraham's adventure

in faith. He had every reason to stagger, but he did not. His body was dead and there was no life in Sarah's womb either. But this man, Abraham, applied the Word rightly.

As Abraham's seed, you have to take your place as one who is following the steps of his father. Abraham believed God and it was credited to him for righteousness (Romans 4:22). Abraham was a believing father; likewise, we ought to be believing offspring.

Notice that each of those fathers who walked closely with God had no symptom of sickness during their entire life time. Abraham's case is obvious.

At the age of 120, Moses had all his system functioning accurately —his eyes were not dim, neither was his natural strength abated (Deuteronomy 34:7). His life was not jeopardised by sickness. He had his strength intact.

People like Jacob, Joseph, and the other patriarchs were people who had nothing to do with sickness in their bodies.

The healthy and successful living of Job

attracted special attention from the devil. He told God that He (God) had built a hedge around Job, and that was why it was easy and convenient for Job to serve Him. Therefore, it implies that one of the hedges God built around His people then was divine health.

The devil was jealous of it. He murmured, grumbled and complained to God about it. Bless God, that hedge is still around us today. It is too strong for the devil to penetrate. It does not matter what he thinks about it. God has spoken and has made a hedge around you.

The counsel of the Lord alone shall stand forever. If God says anything to you in His Word, take time to do it diligently and the result will come.

The prophet Elisha told Naaman to wash in the Jordan seven times if he wanted his leprosy cleansed. That man got angry, but the prophet had spoken. If he had not obeyed, nothing would have happened to the leprosy. However, he obeyed and he was healed, just as the prophet had said.

On another occasion, the sons of the prophet

went out felling trees. Suddenly, the axe-head fell into the river. They screamed and complained to the prophet, Elisha. They even told him the axe-head was borrowed, to show how desperate they were. Elisha asked them to bring a wood, not a hook! And it did the job. The axe-head floated and they recovered it.

It does not really matter what God asks you to do in His Word. The important thing on your side is obedience to that Word. Do not calculate and speculate on how it will work out. Apply it according to prescription and you will get the results. If only you can believe God, you will see His glory of divine health.

You must come to a place of faith in God and His Word so that whatever you see around you does not move you. If you have been sick and you believe God now for your healing, you do not need to wait for the manifestation before you testify of it. The moment you believed; it was done. Seeing is not believing; believing is seeing. That is the law of faith. Believe first, then you will see it come to pass.

Faith is a winner any day, any time. It never gives up. Faith wins the final round in any battle. You do not need to see it before you know it has happened.

> ***Now faith is the substance of things hoped for, the evidence of things not seen.***
>
> *Hebrews 11:1*

Do not depend on your five senses —sight, taste, touch, smell, and hearing to receive a miracle. It does not and will not come that way. Depend on your sixth sense—faith. That is the only sure way to victory over the assaults of the enemy. Say, 'Even if I do not see it now, it does not make any difference. I know it is there. God has said it and I receive it!'

When Jesus cursed the fig tree, there is no record that any physical thing happened to that tree at that time. Thomas must have taken particular interest in what was going on. He must have giggled and pinched one of the disciples, and one of them must have cautioned him to be careful. 'You know He operates the word of knowledge: He can easily know what is going on in your mind'. I believe they persuaded the Lord Jesus Christ to come back through that same route, so that they would be able to confirm the situation of the tree.

Peter called out, ...*Master, behold, the fig tree which thou cursedst is withered away* (Mark 11:20-21). To Jesus, this was no news. He was not excited about it. He knew it happened the moment He spoke the Word, not when it became obvious to the eyes.

The moment you believe God for your miracle, start giving the testimony. It may be foolish to people around you, but the fact is that the wisdom of this world is foolishness to God and the foolishness of God is wiser than the wisdom of man. Faith is not governed by conventional rules. It is governed by the application of God's wisdom— believe and say it before you see it.

God said, you are healed, the symptoms notwithstanding. Be 'foolish' enough to act like it is true. This is what it means to walk by faith. You do not give in to the things your physical senses tell you of your situation. You believe what God said.

> ***(For we walk by faith, not by sight:)***
>
> *2 Corinthians 5:7*

Take this literally; we do not walk by sight. We walk by faith in the unseen. It means you are blind spiritually if you are not walking by faith. If you walk with your sense of sight, you are blind. You will stumble against anything that comes your way. You cannot walk straight without an aid. But when you walk by faith, you walk and see very clearly.

You see like Abraham and the patriarchs saw. This is why Abraham could run at the age of 99. He had his eyes of faith very clear. He could see clearly. He walked by faith and ran by it also. You will not only walk; you will run if you walk by faith. It is over to you.

God intends absolute health for you, but it must come by uncompromising faith in His Word.

A woman got hold of this truth. She was ministered to in the name of the Lord Jesus Christ, and apparently nothing happened to improve her situation and it was obvious to all. But this woman started giving her testimony day and night. She would stand boldly in every church service to testify of her miraculous healing.

She was serious about it. She believed what she was saying. She knew it to be true. She testified of her healing daily, with the sickness still physically obvious. She was not looking at the physical situation. She was walking by the eyes of faith, which saw beyond what was visible to sight. It was during this process that the sickness disappeared. It did not happen when it did physically. It happened the day she believed and was ministered to.

One of the areas the Lord moved me, into when I became a Christian was the life of faith. I concentrated all my reading and studies on the gospels. I loved seeing Jesus saying a thing and healing people. It so caught my attention that I was not interested in any other thing.

The words and works of Jesus so got into me that I did not need to wait for a thing to happen before I announced it. I could not wait.

On one occasion, when I was in school, I gave a testimony of my success in an exam I had just finished. I could not wait for the results. I said God told me. What I was doing was identifying myself with faith. I knew the result before it happened. If I could publicly and boldly declare what God said, I would become the possessor of it. It is the same with you. Declare it! Confession brings possession.

The Shunammite woman is a classical example of faith. She had just lost her child. She went up to the hill to meet the man of God, Elisha. Elisha sent his servant to meet her and ask her about her situation, her husband and her child, and her answer was 'It is well'.

> ***Run now, I pray thee, to meet her, and say unto her, Is it well with thee? Is it well with thy husband? is it well with the child? And she answered, It is well.***
>
> *2 Kings 4:26*

That is Bible faith. People were waiting for her back there in the village, to arrange the burial activities of her son; but she was not prepared for any such thing and heaven commended her faith. The child was raised back to life.

She did not go about complaining or giving situation reports. Those are not relevant in the matter of faith. What actually matters is: has God said a thing concerning it? It does not matter what the problem is, the moment you receive the Word in your heart, it is settled. This is what you need to make divine health a reality. It is all the truth. God's Word is truth.

Jesus is the basis of all truth. He is the Chief Cornerstone.

> ***For other foundation can no man lay than that is laid, which is Jesus Christ.***
>
> *1 Corinthians 3:11*

What Jesus said, did and lived is the foundation for our lives. It is the whole truth about our situation. Take time to study the life of Jesus from the gospels; then look at your foundation, look at what happened there and apply it to yourself. He is the Chief Cornerstone.

The Bible says the apostles and prophets are also the foundation and we are the building. We are built up as spiritual house. These things are written for our example.

> ***For whatsoever things were written aforetime were written for our learning, that we through patience and comfort of the scriptures might have hope.***
>
> *Romans 15:4*

It is recorded of the Lord Jesus Christ that His life was perfect in all forms. He did not know sickness in His body. Peter, James, John and the rest of the apostles did not know it either. They are written for our sake, as an example to emulate, of people who through faith and patience received the promise of divine health. Their bodies were immune to sickness. They are our examples.

The first century Church was a super-church. Sickness was foreign to them. If any man happened to be sick, they could easily know why, because it was not common.

> ***And they continued stedfastly in the apostles' doctrine and fellowship, and***

in breaking of bread, and in prayers.

Acts 2:42

In addition to continuing in the Word, they also continued in fellowship. Many believers have not discovered the importance of fellowship. It is not another coming together of people; it is different from mere gathering. Most of the meetings the Church has held up till now are mere gatherings! 'They continued steadfastly in fellowship'. Most people view and approach fellowship with levity and indifference.

When we come together in fellowship, we are gathered unto Jesus. Wherever people of God are assembled, He is divinely present to heal. He is present there with His virtue and power. He is there in glory and majesty. He is there to bless. The Word says whenever people come together in His name, He is there.

For where two or three are gathered together in my name, there am I in the midst of them.

Matthew 18:20

Our fellowship is with Him. He was ministering somewhere in the scriptures and the power of God was present to heal. The whole atmosphere was charged with anointing for healing.

> ***And it came to pass on a certain day, as he was teaching, that there were Pharisees and doctors of the law sitting by, which were come out of every town of Galilee, and Judaea, and Jerusalem: and the power of the Lord was present to heal them.***
>
> *Luke 5:17*

Understand that when we come together in fellowship, we have not come to a building or a particular preacher. Hebrews 12:22 says we have come to Mount Zion, not to a building. It is to Zion, the city of the living God. We have come to fellowship with God and the spirits of just men made perfect —spirit, soul, and body.

> ***But ye are come unto mount Sion, and unto the city of the living God, the heavenly Jerusalem, and to an innumerable company of angels,***
>
> ***To the general assembly and church of the firstborn, which are written in***

heaven, and to God the Judge of all, and to the spirits of just men made perfect, And to Jesus the mediator of the new covenant, and to the blood of sprinkling, that speaketh better things than that of Abel.

Hebrews 12:22-24

This is a great gathering. It is a mysterious assembly, more mysterious than any mystery in the world. It is superior to all cults anywhere in the world. That is what fellowship is. They continued with faithfulness. So, they were constantly renewed in strength and in health.

They go from strength to strength, every one of them in Zion appeareth before God.

Psalm 84:7

By continuing to fellowship in Zion before God, they moved from strength to strength (health to health)! There is virtue in being in God's presence. The Bible admonishes us not to forsake the fellowship of God's people (Hebrews 10:25). The fellowship place is God's service station for our total health.

The angels are not present for nothing. They are there on active service. They surround them that fear the Lord, to deliver them from their afflictions. Know this and have faith in the possibilities in being in fellowship with God and His people. If you know this, and anchor your faith in it, you will go from strength to strength.

Sometime in 1979, I was so sick I could not stand for five minutes without support. I could not even wave down a taxi. Suddenly, it occurred to me that I should go to the fellowship with the little strength I had in me. Then, I began to boast, saying, 'You weakness, all of you, follow me to where I am going'. I got to the fellowship and took my seat. It was an all-night prayer meeting. The pains seemed to multiply and my strength seemed to give way.

At this point, the leader came to me and said, 'I am sorry, brother David, I did not inform you before that you were going to lead this meeting, please come over'. As he talked, I adjusted my seat and listened to him. Every part of me rebelled in pain. 'No problem', I said, and took my place.

When I started to speak, I said, 'Let us worship the Lord God Almighty'. At this point, I turned backing the brethren, and quoted Hebrews 12:22-24. After finishing, I said, 'I cannot see the name of the devil on the roll'. I knew he was the author of what was happening to me.

The moment the Zion revelation came to me, I knew I was the strongest man there. Strength began to flow into me to the glory of God. I took advantage of fellowship. That is where deliverance, healing, and divine health dwell.

> ***But upon mount Zion shall be deliverance, and there shall be holiness; and the house of Jacob shall possess their possessions.***
>
> *Obadiah 1:17*

One day, we were in the office singing and worshipping, not knowing that one of our staff, who had been very sick before, was having a chronic attack that morning. He did not tell us because we do not hear such reports. But as we went on singing, he said it was as if some thread was being loosened from his system and he was immediately relieved. He knew when the last thread was out. This brother is still okay today. He got it in Zion.

When you come to fellowship, you are coming to the mountain of lovingkindness and mercy, healing and health, love and grace, and everything that makes for life and godliness. If you want to be one of the strong believers, you must appear in Zion on a constant basis, because they that appear in Zion go from strength to strength.

This is one of the secrets of the apostles' divine health. So, James could ask, as if to find out, if it was likely that somebody was sick. The secret of health in the wilderness was the presence of the Rock, which is Christ (1 Corinthians 10:4). They were always in His presence—in fellowship with Him for 40 years.

Another secret of the early Church is that they continued steadfastly in breaking of bread. Notice that the Word says, 'They continued steadfastly in the apostles' doctrine, in fellowship, breaking of bread and in prayers'. They were always holding Communion services.

That is another place of maintaining your divine health. In John 6:53-58, Jesus gave the people a comprehensive teaching on this subject. He told them specifically that if anybody would eat His body and drink His blood, he would enjoy the same life He had, including divine health.

> ***...Except ye eat the flesh of the Son of man, and drink his blood, ye have no life in you.***
>
> ***Whoso eateth my flesh and drinketh my blood, hath eternal life; and I will raise him up at the last day.***
>
> ***For my flesh is meat indeed, and my blood is drink indeed.***
>
> ***He that eateth my flesh, and drinketh my blood, dwelleth in me, and I in him.***
>
> ***As the living Father hath sent me, and I live by the Father: so he that eateth me, even he shall live by me.***
>
> *John 6:53-57*

We need to be consistent partakers of the body and blood of the Lord to keep living in divine health. He said we cannot operate like He did until that life is transfused into us. If the apostles and the early Church needed it, then we need it too.

Oral Roberts broke down after a hectic preaching engagement one day. The first thing he wanted was the body and blood of the Lord. He called on one of his associates to administer the Communion to him, for an inflow of life, energy and health.

Many people have not understood this. They only see the Holy Communion as a fulfilment of one of the sacraments—a mere obedience to the Scriptures. It has become a ritual. But Jesus said, whosoever takes part in it shall live by Him. That is, he shall manifest the same life that is in Him. Therefore, take it in faith!

You need faith in the Communion. The apostles had faith in it. They got it well and got the results. They became embodiments of healthy living by it.

When you take the Communion, you are

showing forth the reason He died. You are remembering everything He did. You are showing and proving to the world the efficacy of His death in your life as a believer.

> ***And when he had given thanks, he brake it, and said, Take, eat; this is my body, which is broken for you: this do in remembrance of me.***
>
> ***After the same manner also he took the cup, when he had supped, saying, This cup is the new testament in my blood: this do ye, as oft as ye drink it, in remembrance of me.***
>
> ***For as often as ye eat this bread, and drink this cup, ye do shew the Lord's death till he come.***
>
> *1 Corinthians 11:24-26*

He died to take our sickness and pains. He came to make us healthy and strong. This is what we are proving and confirming, when we take the Communion. It is a sure way of enriching our health firmly. This divine health has to be made manifest in us. It has to be made plain and clear to all that we are in health, because we live by the Lord Jesus Christ. Show the effect of His death in healthy living.

Look at the apostles once again. They stayed healthy because of these reasons. The problem with many people is that they want these old-time results, but are not ready to do the old-time things. They want old time anointing and health, but shy away from old-time principles. There is no shortcut to it. Take the proper steps to get the desired results.

> ***Thus saith the LORD, Stand ye in the ways, and see, and ask for the old paths, where is the good way, and walk therein, and ye shall find rest for your souls...***
>
> *Jeremiah 6:16*

Get into those old-time principles and you will get the results. That is wisdom.

8

How to Maintain your Divine Health

There is no shortcut to divine health. There are basic rules to it. If we must get divine health, we must faithfully follow the rules with determination and zeal.

God has done everything possible for us to be in health. That is why Jesus came. God is not the author of sickness; the devil is, and he is still planning and devising new diseases and releasing them into the world. You should know your right to health and insist on it.

Christianity is not a religion. It is the supernatural ability to live like God here on earth. If this is not real to you, you must get it right now. Anything that draws you away from the Word of God is your own killer disease. It is trying and struggling to squeeze life out of you.

The Word is the source of your life. If you are cut off from it, you are removed from the source of life, and that will kill you fast.

Many people handle the Word with levity. They allow their Word study to be interrupted anyhow. This is not profitable for you.

Look at the example of Mary and Martha. Martha gave herself to cooking, while her sister sat at the feet of the Master to learn. The Lord told her, 'One thing is needful: and Mary hath chosen that good part'. Simple!

The better part is to listen to the Word at all available opportunities. Do not miss it. Stay where the Word is being preached. It is not how long you have been a Christian that matters, but how much you have in you.

You need to get acquainted with God through studying and hearing the Word. This will be your sure anchor in life. God did not create you a struggler. He created you for victory.

For you to maintain your health, you must be in faith. Have a victory mentality and let the Word of God become your identity. Be willing to accept the Word as you receive it from God.

> ***If ye be willing and obedient, ye shall eat the good of the land:***
>
> *Isaiah 1:19*

Another translation says,

> ***If you will only let me help you, if you will only obey, then I will make you rich (in health, in prosperity, in abundance of everything).***
>
> *The Living Bible (Paraphrased)*

Perilous times are ahead (Paul said at these times, perils will abound). What you are doing now is securing yourself properly before the times come.

Health is going to be precious, appreciable and enviable in our days, that anyone who has it will be looked upon as a king. Now is your time to get ready for it.

It will not be in your favour if you begin to run helter-skelter when troubles come. You need to fortify yourself against evil times, because they will surely come. The Bible says, if you fail in the time of trouble, then your strength is little. You do not need to wait for the trouble before you get ready. Stay in health. Build the Word into your system and it will keep you in health.

The basic foundation for divine health is found in Acts 2:42; Proverbs 4:20-24; Hebrews 12:22-24. We shall preach the gospel of Jesus with divine health.

Take note of these ten ways of maintaining your divine health.

Faith

Our faith must constantly be in working form. We must not relax our faith. It is in direct conflict with the devil. That is what we use in quenching all the fiery darts of the devil. It is what we use in resisting the devil. It is a fight of faith.

> ***Be sober, be vigilant; because your adversary the devil, as a roaring lion, walketh about, seeking whom he may devour:***

Whom resist stedfast in the faith...

1 Peter 5:8-9

Do not wait for disease before putting your faith to work. Be in faith always. That is one way you can keep sickness off your body.

Fasting

This is another weapon. Many Christians think fasting is optional. Jesus did not give that impression. He said, 'When ye fast', not 'If ye fast'. It means fasting is for every believer. It is part of the Christian walk.

There is a time you deliberately have to refuse feeding your body, so that you can take time to attend to spiritual matters. God Himself chose fasting as a means of getting things done (Isaiah 58:6-7). Jesus said, *Howbeit this kind goeth not out but by prayer and fasting* (Matthew 17:21). Jesus Christ Himself fasted. If He did, we should also. It is not just doing away with food; it is leaving food to be with God. It is a spiritual activity that should have all our concentration.

It does not necessarily mean our whole attention is on health. We may not even have health on our prayer list but your fasting and attending to spiritual things— studying the Word, praying and praising will service our physical bodies and renew our strength (Isaiah 40:31).

If you have ever really given yourself to prayer and fasting, you will notice the refreshing that follows. You feel light. Your health comes back to you with new vigour.

> ***Is not this the fast that I have chosen? to loose the bands of wickedness, to undo the heavy burdens, and to let the oppressed go free, and that ye break every yoke?***
>
> ***Then shall thy light break forth as the morning, and thine health shall spring forth speedily: and thy righteousness shall go before thee; the glory of the LORD shall be thy rereward.***
>
> *Isaiah 58:6, 8*

> ***But they that wait upon the LORD shall renew their strength; they shall mount***

> ***up with wings as eagles; they shall run, and not be weary; and they shall walk, and not faint.***
>
> *Isaiah 40:31*

These are fasting days. It keeps our bodies in shape.

Diligence

This is very important. A lot of people are sick and weak because they are lazy and idle. It is commonly said that the devil finds work for the idle hand. If you are always lazing around, the devil will affect you. He will strike you at a time you do not expect.

There is a place for hard work in maintaining our divine health. It is obvious that an unused and uninhabited building rots away easily. Your body is God's building. You are not to leave it idle without hard work.

> ***By much slothfulness the building decayeth; and through idleness of the hands the house droppeth through.***
>
> *Ecclesiastes 10:18*

This does not mean spiritual work alone. It is both ways —spiritual and physical. God does not intend for anyone to be lazy. He expects us to get involved in doing something. He said, 'Do your own work'.

And that ye study to be quiet, and to do your own business, and to work with your own hands, as we commanded you;

1 Thessalonians 4:11

God wants you to contribute to maintaining your divine health through hard work. Do not complain about work. It will help your system. This is quite important. When you have worked hard, your sleep will be sound and sound sleep will help your system to improve.

The sleep of a labouring man is sweet, whether he eat little or much...

Ecclesiastes 5:12

It is a basic physical and spiritual law.

Wisdom

Wisdom is another important point we have to note. It is indispensable in all areas of our lives. In fact, wisdom is indispensable in anything we are set to do. It is the principal thing in all life matters. If you ignore it, you will most definitely run into difficulties.

> ***Be not over much wicked, neither be thou foolish: why shouldest thou die before thy time?***
>
> *Ecclesiastes 7:17*

Hard work must be merged with wisdom. You do not need to overwork yourself unnecessarily. Wisdom is essential here. The Bible says that through wisdom a house is built. We can safely say a house is destroyed through foolishness!

Confession

Proverbs 4:24 says, you should put a froward mouth and perverse lips away from you. Speak health always. Do not acknowledge sickness in your body. Declare boldly. The Word of God spoken in faith from the heart is a creative force.

> ***For I will give you a mouth and wisdom, which all your adversaries shall not be***

able to gainsay nor resist.

Luke 21:15

Speak it loudly, and with boldness.

Love

This is very important. You need a large heart to love the brethren. This will definitely work to your own advantage. You are not losing anything by loving. Everybody, who is acceptable to God, should be acceptable to you too. This love will help you overcome lots of difficulties in your life.

We know that we have passed from death unto life, because we love the brethren. He that loveth not his brother abideth in death.

Whosoever hateth his brother is a murderer: and ye know that no murderer hath eternal life abiding in him.

1 John 3:14-15

Holiness

There is no way you can persist in sinful

habits and expect to be in divine health. It is part of the terms of the covenant. If you are not serving Him in holiness and purity of life, you cannot expect Him to minister divine health to you.

> ***But if, while we seek to be justified by Christ, we ourselves also are found sinners, is therefore Christ the minister of sin...***
>
> *Galatians 2:17*

> ***...Shall we continue in sin, that grace may abound?***
>
> ***God forbid...***
>
> *Romans 6:1-2*

Grace for divine health cannot flourish in an atmosphere polluted with sin. Sin brought sickness, so sin must completely give way if divine health is expected to permeate your body.

Holy Communion

This sacrament is a way of showing faith in the finished work of Christ in our health. As often as you do it, you show the world, and confirm in your body that Christ has taken your grief and sorrow in His body and His blood is transfused into your veins.

The Holy Spirit

The ministry of the Holy Spirit is more than what many believers think it to be. He is very active in the believer's life. He is the seal of the Godhead in our health. He is the Chief Executive of God's plans and purposes and that includes divine health.

> ***And grieve not the holy Spirit of God, whereby ye are sealed unto the day of redemption.***
>
> *Ephesians 4:30*

> ***...When the enemy shall come in like a flood, the Spirit of the LORD shall lift up a standard against him.***
>
> *Isaiah 59:19*

Fellowship

This is the New Testament Mount Zion, as outlined in Hebrews 12:22-24 and Obadiah

17. It is God's service centre. There, your constant health is guaranteed. Go from strength to strength by appearing before God and His innumerable company of angels in Zion.

Beloved, these truths received and applied accurately will lift you to a place of ever springing health. They will help you to enjoy yourself here on earth and reign in heaven with Christ.

Stay in health NOW and always.

Note

Note

Note

ABOUT THE *Author*

David O. Oyedepo, called to be an Apostle with a mandate to liberate the world through the preaching of the Word of Faith, has for nearly four decades been part of the ongoing charismatic revival sweeping across the African continent today. His faith-based teachings have literarily transformed millions of lives around the world.

He is the Founder and President of the Living Faith Church Worldwide also known as Winners' Chapel International, with a network of thousands of Churches in Nigeria and several other nations across the continents of the world.

Till date, he has published over 90 impactful titles most of which have been translated to major languages of the world such as French, Chinese, Spanish etc. with over twenty million copies in circulation.

He is the Senior Pastor of the Faith Tabernacle, Canaanland, Ota, Nigeria, with a 50,000-seat sanctuary, reputed to be the largest church facility in the world. The church currently runs five services on Sunday morning with over 300,000 worshippers, making her one of the largest church congregations in the world.

His mission has established educational institutions across all levels in Nigeria, with Covenant and Landmark Universities taking large strides towards becoming world class universities.

He is married to Faith and they are blessed with sons, daughters and grandchildren.

Books By Dr David Oyedepo

- Wonders of Kingdom Stewardship
- Following The Path Of The Eagle
- The Exceeding Riches Of His Grace
- Not By Power Nor By Might
- The Turnaround Power Of The Word
- Understanding The Power Of Faith
- The Breakthrough Power Of Vision
- On Eagle's Wings
- The Unlimited Power Of Faith
- In Pursuit Of Vision
- Pillars Of Destiny
- Signs & Wonders Today
- Exploits In Ministry
- Winning The War Against Poverty
- Walking In Dominion
- Possessing Your Possession
- The Wisdom That Works
- Exploits Of Faith
- Anointing For Exploits
- Understanding The Power Of Praise
- Walking In Newness Of Life
- Maximise Destiny
- Commanding The Supernatural
- Winning Invisible Battles
- Success Systems
- Understanding Financial Prosperity
- Success Strategies
- Understanding Your Covenant Right
- Miracle Meal
- Exploring the Riches of Redemption
- Anointing For Breakthrough
- Excellency Of Wisdom
- Breaking Financial Hardship
- The Release Of Power
- Walking In The Miraculous

Books By Dr David Oyedepo

- Satan Get Lost!
- The Winning Wisdom
- Walking In Wisdom
- The Healing Balm
- Manifestations Of The Spirit
- Breaking The Curses Of Life
- Overcoming Forces Of Wickedness
- You Shall Not Be Barren!
- Exploring The Secrets Of Success
- Winning Prayer
- Understanding The Anointing
- Fulfilling Your Days
- Towards Mental Exploits
- Understanding Vision
- Understanding Divine Direction
- The Force Of Freedom
- Born To Win
- The Shower Of Blessing
- Riding On Prophetic Wings
- All You Need To Have All Your needs Met
- Operating In The Supernatural
- Ruling Your World
- Success in Marriage *(Co-authored with Faith Oyedepo)*
- The Blood Triumph
- Keys To Divine Health
- Winning Faith
- Conquering Controlling Powers
- Put Your Angels To Work
- Covenant Wealth
- Keys To Answered Prayer
- Miracle Seed
- The Hidden Covenant Of Blessing

INSIDE VIEW OF

Faith Tabernacle

Dr David Oyedepo is the Founding President of the Living Faith Church Worldwide Inc. and the Senior Pastor of the Faith Tabernacle, a 50,000 capacity sanctuary located in Canaanland, Ota, a suburb of Lagos, Nigeria.

The construction of this gigantic architectural masterpiece was completed within twelve months and dedicated on September 18, 1999, built totally debt-free and without any foreign inputs! To God alone be all the glory.

Today, Faith Tabernacle stands as the home of signs and wonders for men and women all over the world, who keep coming in droves to worship the King of kings and the Lord of lords, Jesus Christ the Son of the Living God.

OUTSIDE VIEW OF FAITH TABERNACLE

OVERVIEW OF FAITH TABERNACLE

Visit our website for more information: www.faithtabernacle.org.ng